Violet Hopes

A Good Tale
Volume 2

A Good Tale

Volume 2

Violet Hopes

An Anthology project

The Countryman © 2014 D C Mills

All Done, Well Done © 2014 David Russell

Small Purple Catalyst © 2014 Suzanne H. Ferris

Alone In The City © 2014 Helen Blenkinsop

Zoe and the Dragon © 2014 Rebecca Lacy

Winning Violets © 2014 Mike Boggia

Turned to Stone © 2014 Arlene Lagos

Shadowdeep © 2014 Alli Vaughan

Violet Berries © 2014 Lynn Johnston

Elta's Folly © 2014 Lynette White

The Echoes of Her Past © 2014 Sylvia Stein

Flames of Red Make Violet Blue © 2014 Randall Lemon

Lothario © 2014 Tom Russell

Something Purple © 2014 Linda J. Pifer

Together © 2014 V. J. M. Christensen

Ol Jon Quil © 2014 Todd Folstad

They Paved Paradise–Didn't They © 2014 Gene Hilgreen

The Luck of the Shamrocks © 2014 Lena M. Pate

Alone? © 2014 Douglas G Clarke

Cover by Julianna Putri, Juliannaputri on fiverr.com

Contact the publisher at, support@agoodtale.com

First Printing, 2014

ISBN 978-1-63427-005-2

To all the authors:
Who accept the challenge each month to write a story based on someone else's prompt
Who take a few unrelated thoughts and turn them into their own
Who thrill us with adventure
Who bring a tear to our eyes or a chuckle and a smile
Who, with about a thousand words, entertain us for a few minutes

To all the authors, new and old, experienced and just starting out, who share their stories with each other each month.

To the authors who decided to include their stories here, to those who choose to pursue other opportunities, and to those who write for themselves.

This book is dedicate to you in thanks for being part of the group.

Table of Contents

Introduction

Violet Hopes is a collection of short stories resulting from the question:

"What do a violet (flower or color), something living turning to stone, ash or dust, and a sweet life have in common?"

Collected here are the results from a group of those authors who took up the challenge.

Eighteen authors

Less than thirty days

Each in a different direction.

From a violet as a harbinger of ill to a beacon of hope. From dust being the end of a sweet life, the begging of one, to an unfortunate side effect.

Join us as we look at how a life can be sweet and violet.

The Countryman
by D C Mills

I always knew that I should be king.

Even when we were boys, it was obvious to me that my brother's claim to the throne was merely an accident of his being born first. Aison was meek, sweet, forever seeking approval and friendship. Love. Too weak to rule.

Not even as king did he endeavour to impose fear and respect in others, to mark his territory, so to speak. He sought alliances, preferred diplomacy to battle. Diplomacy can be useful, of course, honeyed words and gifts to lull the opponent; but never should it be the end, only the means to the true end.

This could not go on: our position was gradually weakened; others saw us as an easy target, land to be conquered. My brother would not listen to me.

So I had to prove my point. I am stronger, more fit to rule.

I did not kill him or have him killed. That would have brought down the wrath of the gods on my head. I merely placed him under house arrest; even let his wife follow him. They told me his brat was killed in the melee, though I never saw the corpse.

For fifteen years, I had it all. The power, the title, the riches. My wife and my daughters adorned their hair with ribbons of the finest Tyrian purple. They wore gold bracelets and pearl earrings. And Akastos grew up to be a handsome heir. I did prove my point.

Then strange things began to happen.

Thunderclouds gathered out of nowhere. White-hot lightning flashed purple against the greenish grey clouds and struck the old olive tree in the courtyard, my favourite shady spot on hot afternoons. The dry wood caught flame, and the whole tree burned down in an instant. Nothing else was struck, and the clouds dissipated and blew away, leaving a clear blue sky. As if nothing had happened. Only my olive tree was gone, reduced to ashes dancing on the breeze.

It had to be an omen. Something bad was coming for me.

There was an old prophecy about me: a man from the country, wearing only one sandal, would bring me down. It was uttered long ago, before I had anything worth bringing down, and for many years, I paid it no heed. But suddenly, it came to my mind.

I had to watch those around me. I knew it was ridiculous: nobody walks around wearing a single sandal. Those who are too poor simply go barefoot. But I had to watch them.

A shepherd came back alone from the pasture, claiming that a lion had attacked the flock. Highly unusual for the time of year. Several sheep were indeed found dead or so badly injured that they had to be slaughtered. The shepherd's boy had been mauled and killed, too. The shepherd was of course interrogated, but found to have done nothing wrong.

And he was wearing both his sandals.

I found myself waking in the nights, plagued by thoughts which had no meaning. Strange ideas came to me. What if my brother's son, Jason, was not killed all those years ago? What if he was whisked away, like a boy in a story, to grow up anonymously and return to avenge his father's ignominious fate? To claim his inheritance and ruin all which I had worked for?

But no, this was surely ridiculous.

I could tell no-one of these thoughts. They would think I was going mad, would find me weak and vulnerable. Not even Akastos could be trusted with the secret: he was too young when it all happened, and knew nothing of his cousin. His dead cousin.

* * *

I arranged a great feast, sacrifices to all of the gods, though I had done nothing wrong. A hundred heifers were to be slaughtered. This would show my generosity to all — gods and men alike.

Even Hera, the old hag, must have her due. It would not do to be at odds with the immortals.

For some reason, the pyre for the burnt-offerings refused to catch. The attendants struggled with the kindling.

A murmur rippled through the crowd and died away. In the ensuing silence, a path opened through their midst, and a young man appeared. Dripping wet and wearing only one sandal.

The sky blackened, the ocean roared in my ears.

The young man walked calmly over the open space in front of the blazing fire. When had it been lit?

'Greetings, uncle Pelias,' he said.

* * *

During the feast, I summoned Jason. I had to send him away before he became a threat to me, before Akastos' admiration for his exotic cousin turned into mutual friendship.

I knew how to get rid of him without seeming to: I re-minded him of the fleece of the golden ram, brought to far-away Aia by our uncle Frixos. This fleece, and its power to bring prosperity to the land, rightly belonged here, and the recent row of misfortunes plainly showed how we needed it.

'I am too old now for heroic journeys,' I said. 'Your country needs you.'

'You are young and as yet unknown to the people,' I told him. 'But if you bring back the Fleece, you will have proved your worth, and they will welcome you as king.'

He acquiesced and immediately set about procuring a ship, gathering a crew.

* * *

This morning, they went away. My relief flowed into hearty emulations of good wishes for their journey and safe return, as I watched them embark and set sail.

He will never return: the journey to the ends of the world is perilous, and the king of Aia has no love for strang-ers. If they make it there alive, he will see to it that they never leave.

I am safe; my position once more secure. I send for Akastos: he is old enough now to be taken further into my confidence, to learn the intricacies of ruling.

But they cannot find him – where is he?

All Done, Well Done

by David Russell

"There, that should do it," exclaimed Lilly, as she put the finishing dots and dashes on her chalk drawing on Granny and Pa's driveway. She had lived there for much of her 7 years, after her mother had given her up for adoption.

Granny called, "Lilly, would you bring in the mail?"

"Okay Granny, but come see my drawing. It's really good," replied Lilly.

"I'll come out there after you bring in the mail," replied Granny.

A moment later, Lilly felt a tap on her shoulder, and heard a voice saying a familiar phrase, "Lilly, you are a fine girl and one of God's children." Then, the light and aura faded, and life returned as it had been.

"Lilly, where's the mail? Please bring it in right now," Granny stated firmly through the open screen of the front door.

"I'm getting it now," informed Lilly.

After being inside a couple minutes, Lilly mentioned the voice, light, and shoulder tap occurrence to Granny. She had told Granny and Pa of its first occurrence last summer, but they seemed to regard it as the imagination of a child. This time, Granny nodded and affirmed Lilly being one of God's finest children. Now, the visitations were occurring weekly rather than sporadic as when first noted by Lilly the previous summer.

"Lilly, you have a letter from Uncle Tod. There may be a little gift from him," informed Granny. Uncle Tod was Granny and Pa's only son and now only child, since Terri, his sister, Lilly's mom, had died in a motor vehicle accident last winter. Tod was in the US Army and had written to them regularly since joining. He was about to finish his 4-year tour.

Lilly read the letter out loud to Granny:

Dear Lilly,

I hope you are having fun this summer. Thank you for the pictures of the flower garden, blooming violets, you, Pa, Granny, monkey and bear. I will be home for your birthday, and after a few days will be moving to a small farm 1 hour away. All of you are free to visit when you can.

By the way, I am sending you another US Savings Bond to add to the others. These will be yours to use after you graduate from the 12th grade. I need to go, but will see you around your birthday.

Love to you, Pa, and Granny,

Uncle Tod

"He's the best uncle, and I love him," Lilly stated with a very wide smile.

"We are all very proud of him, and you too," Granny responded.

Tod had demonstrated interest in Lilly once it was apparent Terri would not continue her role as Lilly's mother. Terri wanted to "live" and single parenting seemed to oppose that desire. By the time Lilly was age 2, her mother was largely gone from all their lives. Strong faith in God coupled with providing for and raising Lilly became consistently Pa and Granny's doing.

A couple days later, Tuesday afternoon, Lilly came home after spending the morning with friends playing at Melanie's house.

She asked while coming in, "Granny, did you just bake some cookies?"

"I did, help yourself to a couple," urged Granny.

"Can I take a bag of them to the play group tomorrow," asked Lilly.

"You can, just put them in a big enough zip-lock bag for everyone," advised Granny.

On Wednesday afternoon, the play group of about 10 to 12 youngsters met up at the Court Street pool. The youngsters were supervised by both Mrs. Karlson and Mrs. Wilson.

"You need to buddy up before you go in. Find a buddy," instructed Mrs. Wilson.

Lilly and her classmate Violet were swim partners for the time at the pool. The mood overall was fun and playful.

"OMG, Billy has a big zit on his back, yuck," exclaimed Violet.

Just then both girls saw a bright light, felt a shoulder tap and heard a voice gently but clearly state, "God loves you both." Then it ceased and life returned as it had been. Both girls smiled and Lilly quickly added, "This happens to me often, but glad you were part of it Violet."

After a half hour more, the kids were instructed to come out for a snack , and all enjoyed the baked cookies brought by Lilly. Then they were driven home in the SUV, and informed they would be going to a movie next week at the theater.

Two nights later, the family had turned in, but in the night each had the same dream where an angel told them Lilly would be going to heaven a few days after her birthday. She is needed there to serve as an angel watching over family and friends here on earth. The next morning over

French Toast, they talked about the dream, that this would be a good thing if it occurs, and enjoy the time they now have together.

The night before Lilly's 8th birthday, August 24, Tod arrived home. They enjoyed dinner and family time. He was told of the dream and was overall supportive and in agreement with what it may mean.

"Lilly, Lilly, -- Lilly, get up. It's 8:00 and you are 8," exclaimed Pa outside Lilly's bedroom door.

"We are having pancakes and then picking up Violet to go to the water park," informed Pa.

As the day advanced, each had decided to enjoy it to the fullest and did, ending with dinner at Ruby Tuesdays late that afternoon before going home.

On the last night of August, everyone had turned in after a day of walking and playing at the local school playground. Around 2:30 a.m., an angel gently approached, called to Lilly, and escorted her to heaven, directly to God's loving presence.

"Lilly, it's you," stated her Mumma. They hugged for a long time and cried happy tears. It was a joyous reunion. Lilly lived as an angel, and lived in the memories of all who knew and love her.

Small Purple Catalyst

by Suzanne H. Ferris

Her mind drifted back to the wheat field outside their house, the house where she'd grown into a gangly ten-year-old, awkward knees and elbows always bruised from knocking into corners that had been further away the day before.

Emyra and her father had been walking Rusty, the black and white collie they'd owned back then.

"Look, Dad." She'd stooped and plucked a flower nodding under the fence towards the road.

"It's a lonely violet, trying to break free from the wheat," her father replied. "Let's take it home and give it to your mother."

She stared at that violet when they returned home, when her father opened the door, walking down the hall calling for her mother. The noise he made when he opened the kitchen door stayed in Emyra's head, sounding there even now, when on the odd occasion she allowed vulnerability a chance to torment her.

Her father had shepherded her into the living room, shut the door, leaving her staring at the drooping violet. But, all that had been a long, long time ago.

When Emyra was 25 years old she looked in the mirror at her long hair for the last time. She was almost a bride and long hair had no place competing with a veil.

"Why do you want it cut, honey?" The stylist lifted a haft of pale yellow hair. "It's so beautiful. What I wouldn't give to have hair this colour, rather than my frizzy mousy-mess."

The long hair fell to the hair-salon's mint-green floor. Adjusting her neck to its lightened load, Emyra's gaze in the mirror fell upon a shelf at the rear of the salon, a shelf supporting a glass jar full of violets, and she sucked in a breath.

"What is it, honey? You regretting the cut already?"

Emyra heard the noise; every person in the town must have heard it. A mind-numbing boom that rang through your very soul. A gas explosion, they said. It was no-one's fault. These things just happened. But, it had happened to her man, her groom-to-be, Fergus.

Of course she still married him. Emyra heard the whispers it was a pity wedding, but she wasn't the sort to leave. Fergus was a shell of his former self, a husk, a useless reminder of what he used to be. She watched him slowly wither away in his chair, the wheels creaking on the porch each time the wind blew in across the fields of wheat.

He died on a Sunday, God's day, and she was glad he'd seen fit to eventually take Fergus back; God should have taken him a long time ago rather than leaving him to stare into the middle distance thinking whatever thoughts rampaged through his tortured mind. Fergus had never voiced his thoughts, and heck, Emyra wasn't sure she'd have wanted to listen if he had. But Fergus was gone now. Safe with God.

She didn't know why she did it, but she did. The house sold, the ticket bought, Emyra just wanted to leave the wheat fields far behind. She boarded the bus, put her forehead on the window-glass and slept for several hundred miles, waking only when they reached the first border. Flickering her sleepy eyes, Emyra looked at the distant hills, they didn't have many hills where she came from, and she yawned, deep and long.

"I thought you were never going to wake." The woman sitting next to Emyra put down her knitting and smiled. "I was watching you, waiting for signs of a breath, but you were like the dead. Recharging, were you?" The woman executed a wink, the crinkles round her eye closing like a fan.

"Something like that." Emyra attempted a smile, not something she was good at.

"Going far?"

"As far as it takes."

And it had been good. Life had carried her to a town by a lake, bigger than what she'd been used to. She'd met a man, never married him, she didn't want to take the risk. But they'd been happy. They'd managed no kids, distracting themselves with dogs.

"Come on, Gyp," she said, tugging on the leash. "We've got to get back and give Doug his breakfast, you know how he can't start his day without bacon."

She stopped where she stood, staring at the clump of violets, the dark glossy green leaves, the purple flowers waiting behind a rock.

Emyra sucked in a long breath. She looked at her hand, she looked at the dog, she thought of Doug.

Alone In The City

by Helen Blenkinsop

"Just tap water, please. I'm waiting for someone."

The waitress' heavily made-up eyelids flicker, as if she knows it's a lie. But the water is brought to him, in a tall glass on a silver tray, with ice and lemon.

He takes the pristine pack of Silk Cut out of his pocket, and examines it. White, silver and violet. Pure and light. As British as a cup of tea in the afternoon. His American colleagues used to rib him about it, guzzling quarts of Diet Coke with ice and smoking Marlboro. What do they put in those things, the American brands? Vanilla, chocolate, caramel, he read somewhere. Comforting, sweetshop flavours. No wonder they hook children.

And yet… He remembers when he spent pocket money on cigarettes, pooling resources with his friends and splitting the packet between them. The taste wasn't important. What mattered was looking and feeling cool, and yes, the pleasure as nicotine coursed through his bloodstream. No surprise, then, that adults told you not to do it; they wanted to keep all the fun for themselves.

Eight quid a packet they cost now, though. How can schoolkids afford it? He struggles to pay for the habit himself. Twenty a day. Over fifty pounds a week. He bought some bootleg last month; three pounds a pack from a man outside a pub, it should have been a bargain. It looked the real deal too. Of course, it wasn't. The sticks inside the perfect packaging were quick to burn, rough on the back of his throat. He smoked two before he threw them away in disgust, gave them away to a beggar, actually, and with relief, handed over the usual extortionate sum to his smiling newsagent the next morning.

He won't buy more, though. The overdraft and credit card maxed out, his landlord about to sling him out after two months without rent, redundancy money spent and no work on the horizon.

He sips the iced water, lights a cigarette, looks across the roof garden to the City beyond. The Bank of England and Royal Exchange sit sedate and confident, cloaked in white marble, dwarfed by the Johnny-come-lately glass towers behind them. Who controls the City? He shudders, suspecting computer algorithms singing in a faraway place, New York, or perhaps Shanghai, and traders like himself dancing to their tune.

Or traders sharper, shinier than him. "We see smoking as a weakness," he was told, when he was asked to clear his desk. "A sign of that you can't handle stress, that you're about to crack."

He feels a sense of anti-climax. After all the years trading, earning big and spending bigger, what's left? He felt the same when, as a kid, he and Benny played for two hours on House of the Dead in the local arcade. That's right, two hours. There was a glitch in the machine; it kept giving them credits for free. And guess what? After two hours of adrenaline-pumped shooting, they actually ran out of zombies. He and Benny shot them all.

"Are you all right, sir?"

The waitress again. She's noticed how close he is to the parapet.

"You should sit down, sir. I expect your friend will be here soon." She leads him through the crowds to a table. Perhaps she can see him wrestling demons within, has been trained to spot suicide risks. There have been other leaps over the wall here lately.

He thought he knew what he came here for, but as he flicks ash aside, the nicotine is starting to kick in, clearing his head. The certainty of a very grim, but swift future vaulting over the parapet, begins to fade. Instead, he faces the uncertainty of a slow future without cash. His mother in Yeovil would take him back, past arguments and lack of work in Yeovil notwithstanding. He sighs. He must swallow his pride even more, ask his City friends if he might couch-surf, take bar work – anything. Use e-cigarettes. Smoking has been modernised, entering the virtual world where zombies are vanquished and fortunes lost in a flash.

There are still choices. Contemplating them, alone among the chattering crowds, he lights another of his last cigarettes.

Zoe and the Dragon

by Rebecca Lacy

Zoe and Chuck are unlikely best friends. Zoe is a dreamer who pretends to ride a sparkling white unicorn with an amethyst horn rather than her bike. She even tapes long streamers of ribbons to her helmet, making it into a damsel hat.

Chuck, on the other, prefers to live in the real world where everything can be logically explained. His idea of make believe is sheriff versus gun slinger of the old west, where there was no confusing good and evil.

The two love to play in the woods near their neighborhood. For Zoe, it is the Black Forest, filled with magical creatures and witches ready to cast a spell on unsuspecting children, and where the bridges are excellent hiding places for trolls and other unsavory folks. Chuck sees the forest as the perfect place for a sworn enemy of the law to hide from justice. To him, the deer and raccoons that he tracks through the woods are really the footsteps left by notorious crooks. Sometimes their two worlds crisscross when one of

Chuck's master criminals kidnaps one of Zoe's fair maidens, and the friends are required to work together to free her and bring the villain to justice.

During a visit to the woods one August day, they were walking down a trail looking for adventure when a rabbit ran out of the bushes in front of them. Suddenly an enormous bird swooped down, plucked up the poor animal, and carried it off.

Chuck and Zoe ran through the forest in the direction that the bird had flown. When they came to a clearing, they saw the giant bird flying overhead, its prey clutched in its talons. Zoe had a lump in her throat, realizing that there was little chance that they would be able to rescue the rabbit. As she watched with a feeling of hopelessness, she saw something that looked like a puff of smoke. The bird let out an angry shriek, and it released its prey, letting it plummet toward earth earthward. Without a thought, Zoe rushed to catch it. The thing about wild animals is that they aren't always grateful when they are rescued. Such was the case for Zoe's catch.

"Ouch! That hurt!" Zoe exclaimed, dropping the animal, which scurried into the bushes.

"Did it bite you?" asked Chuck. "Maybe it has rabies."

"No, it burned me," she said as Chuck came closer to examine her injury.

"How could a rabbit burn you?"

"I don't know what it is, but that isn't a rabbit. Where did it go?"

It didn't take long for them to track where the animal had gone, under some shrubs to hide. Zoe got down on all fours to look for it. What she saw looking back at her from under the bush amazed her. "Chuck, it's a dragon!"

"C'mon, quit fooling around."

"Really, it's a dragon."

Chuck knelt down to get a look for himself. "What is… What's that thing?" he yelled, jumping to his feet.

"I told you it's a dragon…a tiny dragon. Where do you think it came from? It's too little to be on its own."

"Zoe, there's no such thing as dragons, and this is no time for pretending. That thing bit you. It might be poisonous."

"It's not poisonous and it didn't bite me. It burned me."

Seeing that Zoe was planning on pulling the animal out from under the bush, Chuck cried, "Don't touch it."

Ignoring his warning, she picked it up and exclaimed it, "It's just a baby." Once in Zoe's arms, the dragonet struggled for a moment then relaxed.

"Isn't she beautiful?" The dragon's body was a dark violet that flashed with every color of the rainbow when the sun touched her skin.

"Well, what are you going to do with her?"

"We have to find her mother, of course."

"I'll look for tracks. Maybe we can find her that way," Chuck offered.

"And I know just where we should look," Zoe replied, drawing on her knowledge of dragon lore. "Dragons love caves! Her mother probably has a nest in one of the caves in Spirit Canyon."

The two raced through the woods until they reached Spirit Canyon, which was named for the eerie sound that the wind makes when it blows across the caves that dot the canyon wall.

"If this is the right place, Mom Dragon could be watching us right now. She might not be too happy seeing you holding her baby," Chuck advised.

"You're probably right. We better leave her here, and hide in the trees."

As soon as Zoe put her down, the dragonet started complaining loudly. Reluctantly, Zoe ignored her cries and retreated to the shelter of the trees to watch.

Within seconds, a shadow was cast over the clearing. Zoe and Chuck looked up expecting to see the mother dragon, but it was the bird, ready to reclaim its prey. Just as it was about to snatch the baby in its talons, there was a sudden blaze of fire, and the bird disintegrated into a puff of ash.

Before Chuck and Zoe had time to recover from that shock, an enormous dragon landed within feet of where they crouched. It picked the baby up by the nap of her neck, and with a great downward thrust of wings, was airborne. Leaving the shelter of the trees, the friends shielded their eyes as they watched the dragon fly upward, but it quickly disappeared into the sun's glare.

As they rode home Chuck asked, "Are you going to tell your parents what happened today?"

"Are you kidding? They would. They'd. They'd say I was lying and ground me for life."

They agreed that they would never tell a soul about what happened that day, but that didn't stop them from going back to look for the dragons. Every now and then they find some footprints that they can't quite explain, but they have never again seen a dragon.

Winning Violets

by Mike Boggia

Lori bent over the raised flowerbed, on the patio, to examine her violets. The purple flowers filled the air with sweet perfume and brought childhood memories of her upstate New York home.

"Take a closer look, darling." Chad's hand closed around the back of her neck and shoved her face into the flowers and leaves. "You remind me of a bird searching for worms." He laughed and let go.

She smelled the green of the crushed leaves, and straightened.

"You even act like a bird, head cocked to one side." He chuckled.

"Chad, you're mean. It's the only way I can see things."

Macular degeneration has stolen her central vision a few years ago, at an unusually early age. Chad hadn't believe her complaints about her eyes until it was too late for the ophthalmologists to help her. They fought to preserve her remaining sight.

Chad complained about the cost of the injections each time Lori scheduled an appointment with the retina specialist. It wasn't a lack of money. Chad's career as a broker kept him in expensive sports cars and clothing. He never let Lori forget his kindness for putting up with her. Any man in my position should ditch a blind wife, he threatened.

Lori hung her head and sighed. He'd been subtle at taking control of her life after her vision blurred. She was a prisoner in her own home, unless one of her friends took her shopping or to medical appointments. She feared living with, or without him.

"I have a meeting in Paris, Tuesday, little pipistrelle girl. I'll leave tomorrow, be back on Saturday." He turned. "Oh, better wash your face, it's green."

* * *

Lori mixed fertilizer into the soil of the raised flowerbed and planted wild violet seeds. The other beds, ringing the shaded patio, with its seven-foot adobe walls, overflowed with lush violets, in full bloom. The large, purple flowers matched Lori's dress. She caressed the leaves as she walked past them.

That afternoon, she welcomed the Silver Canyon Garden Club. Her violets won first prize for nonnative species in the Sonoran Desert.

Janet, her best friend, accompanied Lori into the kitchen to help carry iced tea to the judges and club members.

"How are you doing, without Chad, the Cad?" Janet placed ice cubes in glasses. "It's over a year."

Lori smiled. "I'm fine. With my sister living a mile away, it's all good."

"I admire your bravery. I'd be lost if James left me. To desert you when you're. . ." Janet blushed and sucked in her breath. "Sorry, I realize you can take care of yourself."

Lori shrugged. "I manage."

"Do the police have any leads?"

Lori shook her head. "He flew to Paris, checked into the hotel, but never arrived at the next day's meeting. By the time the police started searching for him, no traces remained. He withdrew five hundred thousand from our account before he left."

"Another woman?"

"I don't know, Janet. The police think Chad may have been killed, because he was carrying such a large amount of money."

Janet hugged her.

Lori sighed. "I keep hoping he'll come home, or, at least send a lawyer to ask for a divorce."

Janet picked up the pitcher of tea. "I'm here for you."

One of the judges paused on the front step. "I don't know how you do it, Lorie. Those wild violet flowers are the deepest purple I've ever seen and the leaves, so green and lush. What's your secret?"

She winked and stepped close to him. "Oh, Dr. Felder, I just have a green thumb and a special, hand mixed fertilizer."

Lori closed the door on her guests and lifted her glass of tea toward Chad's picture. "Chad, I found Axel, who passed for you, on the internet. After burying you, he assumed your ID. Several months later, he returned, dug up your remains, and pulverized them to dust. Honey, you're the most expensive fertilizer I ever bought, but worth every cent."

Turned to Stone

by Arlene Lagos

I wasn't always this way. Before the attacks, I was very out-going. Social events littered my calendar. There wasn't a person in town that didn't know me. My life was perfect, and then one day, it wasn't. The first attack happened on a Saturday in early December. Not wanting to miss my bus to NYC, I stepped on the gas and sped up towards the station. The sky was grey and I remember feeling it weigh on me.

As I pulled into the parking lot, I felt dizzy; and then a rush of heat flowed through me. My chest began to rise and fall as I struggled to catch my breath. Managing to get a ticket and board the bus, I found a seat towards the middle and sat there, leaning my head against the window and closing my eyes. Perhaps I was just tired, I thought, as the bus pulled out of the station.

The feeling of the bus vibrating on my back caused my breath to quicken again. Heat rushed throughout my body again as beads of sweat formed around my face. Out of nowhere, utter darkness came over me, as if I was going to die at any second. The eerie feeling that something horrible was about to happen caused me to jump from my seat at the next stop and depart the bus.

I ran to the nearest police officers and told them something was wrong, that I was having a heart attack or something. They immediately called an ambulance and brought me to the hospital. They ran test after test to see if I was having heart problems, had a brain tumor, or was pregnant. After the tests were done, the doctor came in and sat down beside my bed. Tears rolled down my face as I anticipated the worst.

"You have what's called Panic Disorder," He said.

Rolling onto my side I clutched the pillow and buried my face in it. Four years as a Psychology major and I didn't even recognize it.

It's been a few years now and every day the depression gets worse. I'm too paralyzed to live my life the way it's meant to be lived because of fear. It feels as if I've been turned to stone, unable to move or enjoy anything. The attacks were so bad that I had become agoraphobic.

Pulling the window shade up, I glance out the window at the hot sun beating down on the burnt grass. It has been a nasty summer from what I've heard, I've spent most of it inside. From the looks of my neighbor's flower garden, everything that was growing there has long since died of thirst. Except for that very beautiful patch of violets. Violets have always been my favorite flower. They remind me of my aunt, who passed away about a month before the attacks came. She always smelled like violets. Running to the closet I grab my binoculars and press them to my face to get a better look. They are exquisite. How I long to smell them again. To be reminded of my aunt whom I miss so much. If only I could make it outside for just a moment, maybe I could pick one and bring it inside. Shaking my head, I pull the shade back down knowing it will never happen.

Walking aimlessly around the house I find myself getting on my shoes and heading for the door. What am I doing? I can't stop. The desire to see the violets up close, to hold them, to smell them is so strong that before I know it I'm standing right over them. Kneeling down, I press my nose against them – inhaling their sweet intoxicating smell. Tears roll down my cheeks as I cry over my aunt's death. For hours I sit there. The sun begins to set and as I look up at the pink sky, something inside of me felts calm, like everything is going to be okay. Looking back at the door to my house I frown; I don't want to go back in. Turning my head down the driveway I felt the road calling my name. Slowly I stand up, picking a violet and placing it behind my ear. The warm summer air blankets me as I begin walking down the driveway and onto the sidewalk, destination unknown. Perhaps wherever I am headed to, I will find myself again at the end of the road.

Shadowdeep

by Alli Vaughan

Shadowdeep Canyon gouged into the terrain like claws had ripped it into being. Dark, even on the brightest summer day, it hoarded noxious plants and ironbrush, a twisted secret, tucked away in shame.

It seemed an appropriate place for three Darkun, Shadow Wolves, to be traveling to tonight.

Vene's eyes spread open like small fissures beneath his dark fur. His black eyes were mists in bare sockets, his mortal eyes long scored, leaving hollow expanses through which the sight vapor rose.

They would not be able to move forward. "Stop, Morday. There's something below," he said nipping at his mate's fur as he drew next to her.

"What would Darkun fear?" she whispered.

Was she challenging him? He studied her. Froth poured from her mouth. The same dark mist Vene boasted also wafted from Morday's empty eyes. Where the blackness flowed before her the plant life shriveled and died. Darkun poison. No vessel in the world could hold the poison except the body of a Darkun.

She didn't meet his gaze nor were her fangs drawn from beneath her cloaked jowl. It wasn't defiance then. It was something else. She was protecting Presence, he realized, glancing at the little hoary pup next to her.

"Not with him," he warned. Morday let out a low howl in response.

"Presence must be named," she said eagerly, licking the pup.

"All ancients will be named," he agreed, "my son above all." Presence shook the fur on his back as a hidden itch irritated his soft skin, taking no note of his parent's serious tones. He concerned himself with a bug he saw on the canyon wall, stalking it until it disappeared into a crack. Presence sniffed the hole then ran back to his parent's side.

"The naming is tonight, Vene, we can't go around," Morday begged.

"I'll decide," he snarled, but grew silent as the creature moved into sight. It moved up from the bottom of the canyon like a mountain pushed in a slow cart, purple and grotesque. Both adult Darkun wolves growled and their black fur bristled.

"It's so big." Presence craned his neck as high as it would go.

"It's been feeding," Vene said.

"What is it?" Presence asked.

"Once an Elemental, now it's nothing more than De-vourer," Vene growled.

"Will you kill it?" Presence asked.

The ground trembled and Vene's every muscle tensed. The Devourer tumbled toward them like a drunkard with choppy steps. "It sees Presence," Morday yipped. Presence cowered behind his mother's fur; his former boldness vanished.

"That way," Vene yelled, biting at his mate's heel and herding her. Morday and the pup sprinted away from the entrance of the canyon out onto the open field as Vene ducked under cover. Missing him, the creature barreled toward the pair. Vene would have to create a distraction.

Vene's seeker mists soared from his eyes and swathed the creature in shroud. Though Vene stood a great distance from the creature, he could see it as if he had climbed up on its great shoulder. He snarled at it, but it ignored him.

Then the creature shrieked with a sound that made even Vene's claws tighten. The living thing sank down smoothly from its upright position into a mass on the ground. Vene paused but didn't advance. The clay seemed to bubble and burst several times as it reformed. Once shaped fully, the devourer lay with four legs sprawled out, in the form of massive wolf, so large it looked like a giant cloud formation. On four legs, the Devourer ripped across the land. It would be on his family in moments if he didn't act now. Vene charged out of the thicket and threw himself at the creature. His claws sliced, but he misjudged the grip and went sprawling into the mud.

Vene rolled back onto all fours and darted after the creature again, his feet slipping on the ground. With all of his strength he jumped upward. He burrowed his claws into the surface, slipping as he scaled the creature. Finally, his claws offered a decent grip and he lowered his head. His teeth sliced into the creature and released a violent flow of venomous toxin.

The Devourer staggered, swaying like a slashed tree. Vene jumped down off the creature and waited for it to collapse, stepping back far enough so it would not come crashing down on his head. Morday and Presence stopped as well, sensing it had been brought to a standstill. The tan clay of the creature turned ash black as it became diseased from within by the Darkun poison.

Morday growled a little as she came close. Presence ran in a few nervous circles at their side as they waited.

"Why isn't it dying?"Morday shouted.

"This is more than a Devourer," Vene answered, wrapping his mist around the staggering creature once more. Vene became immaterial, fading in and out of sight. Driving them like a chariot on fire, he forced his mists further, down through the creatures gaping mouth and into its deep bowels. Vene made contact with something inside and yelped in pain. Ancients didn't feel pain, yet this seared him, burned him from the inside.

"Go!" Vene exclaimed.

This time there was no question; Presence would die if this thing reached him. Morday and Presence ran until they were no more than a thin line in the far horizon. It was just Vene and this thing now.

"Why do you approach me?" he asked. The creature tested its back legs as well, the ash color fading from its exterior as it shed the color like a second skin.

"Devour," the word forced out like wind, rather than spoken. It was clear that the Devourer God was no longer interested in his pup.

Vene jumped at the creature again with a wicked laugh. With a final bite, the Darkun poison emptied fully into the creature and it crumbled to ash. Vene lay down, giving the last of his life for his family.

Violet Berries

by Lynn Johnston

Eight year-old Maggie watched as her mother rolled the vacuum cleaner back into the closet. While wrapping the cord neatly, Mom said, "Your Aunt Sharma is coming to stay with us. I need to get the house spotless. It's a beautiful day Maggie. Run along and play outside."

Maggie never liked her Aunt Sharma. She was too eccentric for her taste. Her aunt's eyes were narrow while her eyebrows came to a point. Her stringy black hair seemed to lack style as it framed her pale boney face. The more Maggie thought about it, the more certain she was that Aunt Sharma must be a witch. She wondered if anyone else suspected, but then her mom seemed to like that strange lady.

While turning the doorknob, her mom reminded her, "And remember don't eat the.."

"Violet berries," Maggie interjected, finishing her mother's sentence. "I know, I know," she added before stepping through the door and promptly pulling it shut. As she ran through the front yard, she tried to recall where she once found some sweet blackberries growing. Heading towards a thicket just beyond her yard, Maggie located the blackberries on the edge of the neighboring woods. Just as before, they were so sweet and juicy. Trying hard to avoid the sharp brambles, she carefully plucked the juicy berries and popped them into her mouth. Maggie resolved that if she couldn't pick the violet berries that grew in the back field, that she would settle for the blackberries.

Yet, she pondered why her mother reminded her almost daily not to pick the violet berries. What was so special about them? The more she pondered the question, the more tempted she was to pick them. "Maybe they're magical." As she continued to question the possibilities, she headed towards the field to take a peek at them.

While walking through the field's tall grass, she turned her head to the unmistakable sound of her Aunt Sharma's car pulling up the driveway. Even from thirty yards away, the popping sound of her jalopy could be heard. The very sight of her faded yellow car made Maggie roll her eyes in disgust. "Perfect!" she exclaimed. "I'll pretend I didn't see her and stay here."

As she rounded the corner of the field, she spotted the beautiful plump violet berries. She gazed at them in awe of their splendor as she tried to imagine their succulent taste. The crunching sound of leaves grabbed her attention, causing her to look for the source of the sound. It was Mr. Davis approaching, her elderly neighbor, who lived directly behind her house. He was a carrying a bucket as he smiled warmly in her direction. "I picked some beans from my garden for your family Maggie."

Mr. Davis was a friendly sort, but a rather odd bird. He would often tell strange tales that she didn't know if she should believe or not. Just the same, she decided to ask him about the berries. "Mr. Davis, my mother has been telling me every day not to pick the violet berries. What's so special about these berries that would make her warn me not to eat them. Are they poisonous?"

"They are more than just poisonous. If you eat just one, you will turn to stone!"

"Huh..." she gasped. "Thanks Mr. Davis." He handed her the bucket of beans and walked away nodding his head.

"Could that really be true?" she speculated as she watched Mr. Davis return to his yard.

Still wanting to wait it out, she lay in the field with her eyes watching the violet berries. Before long a cardinal landed in the field, perched itself on a twig, and ate a violet berry. "Oh no!" she screamed. "Don't eat the berries! They are bad...you'll turn to stone!"

The yelling startled the bird. It retreated into the woods with Maggie chasing after it. She couldn't keep up and quickly lost sight of the fleeing cardinal. Yet, running in panic caused Maggie to end up much further into the woods than she had ever been before. Not sure where to go, she followed a path that lead her to an old fenced yard. Curious, she climbed the fence. Spotting something white in the distance, she kept walking to see what it was. When she was able to identify the white object , she screamed in horror – a stone cardinal!

"It's true!" Gazing about the yard, she saw other creatures that had been turned to stone, a snake and a humming bird among them.

The reality of it was so shocking that Maggie ran at an incredible speed, her adrenaline pumping. She flew into her house, out of breath – facing Aunt Sharma forgotten.

"There you are Maggie!" exclaimed Mom. "Your Aunt Sharma is in the kitchen pulling her special pie out of the oven."

Trying to catch her breath, Maggie was drawn into the kitchen by the tantalizing smell. Feeling embarrassed to have thought so negatively about her aunt, Maggie hugged her graciously with a humbled smile. "That pie looks delicious Aunt Sharma."

"Thank you my dear Maggie...it's called Violet Berry Pie."

Maggie watched Aunt Sharma place the pie on the table. She noticed her wicked smile, then scream uncontrollably and scramble out of the kitchen.

Looking flabbergasted, Mom said, "I can't imagine what's gotten in to her. I told Maggie not to eat the berries so you'd have enough for your pie."

Elta's Folly

by Lynette White

Unlike most flowers that welcomed the sun's light, Moon Dust Flowers wait for the moonlight to show their deep purple faces. The Moon Dust blossom's healing properties are legendary, and their gray colored leaves are dried and used to enhance awareness during sacred druid rituals. Letha Ikmen was the only druid within a week's ride to successfully raise the fragile flowers.

Just one month past her thirteenth birthday, Erianna Ikmen, Letha's daughter, had already proved she was a gifted druid. She could easily bond with the life force of any living thing from a blade of grass to the mighty eagle; feeling their pain, joy, weakness and strength.

Erianna was using the full moon's bright beams and power to tend to a struggling blossom when she heard a argument break out near the house. As she stood, she brushed her thick blond hair from her dirt streaked face. With a sigh, she started toward the house to see what her younger sister has done now to invoke their mother's wrath.

"You will get nothing from me, Elta!" Her mother screamed as Erianna reached the small cluster of trees near the house.

"Oh no, not Elta." Erianna said to herself with a groan and tucked herself behind a tree.

Elta was the only druid her mother openly disapproved of. If she was here it only meant one thing, she sought Moon Dust flowers.

"Why are you being so stubborn, Letha?" said Elta.

"Because you make a mockery of the flower's sacred powers, Elta! You demand money for their healing powers and sneak the leaves into the pipes of innocent men for your own pleasure."

"Lies and accusations!"

"Proven fact is not an accusation, Elta. Now get off my property!"

"You are a fool, Letha!" Elta screamed as she pulled her wand out of the pouch on her hip. "I am done with this constant bickering."

Rika, Erianna's five year old sister, rushed to their mother. Despite thirty years of differences the two older women had never drawn weapons so Letha froze as Elta's cold and angry chant echoed in the air around them. Erianna stood helpless while Letha and Rika screamed in agony as their bodies turned to stone.

"No mother!" Erianna screamed and started toward them, but she stopped when Elta spun around to claim her next victim.

Erianna's tiny frame trembled and her heart raced as she realized the danger she was in. Somehow her panicked mind acknowledged that since her father was not there she was the only hope they had. She forced the fear away. As Elta stalked toward her, Erianna slipped back into the trees. She touched the tree closest to the edge, and begged it to help her.

She waited until Elta reached the edge of the trees, then attacked. The branches shot down and wrapped themselves around Elta and the leaves tightly clamped themselves over her mouth. Elta glared at the young girl with the fierceness of a predator as Erianna gathered her courage. Erianna walked up to Elta and ripped the wand from her hand.

"You should have left when you were told to, Elta," said Erianna, her voice shaking. "Now you have two choices." She paused and when she continued her voice was steadier. "You free my mother and my sister or I tell the branches to squeeze your life from you."

The words Elta screamed back at her from behind the leaves were making the tree very angry. Erianna could feel the other trees giving her their strength and courage.

"Tsk, tsk, Elta, not a wise decision to anger your captor. Now what will it be? Do you leave here a free woman or die in this angry tree?"

Elta's response was to kick at the branches that held her and curse Erianna. The young girl shrugged her shoulders and sighed.

"Have it your way then" she said and touched the tree.

The branches constricted just enough to make Elta panic.

"Now tell me, Elta, will this wand reverse the spell?"

Elta kicked the branches harder, but they held fast.

"I will take that as a yes." Erianna walked to her mother.

Once Erianna reversed the spell, Letha took the wand from her and broke it into three pieces. Her mother beamed with pride as the three of them returned to the tree. Erianna touched the trunk and Elta hit the ground with a hard thud. As Elta struggled to stand up, Letha tossed the useless wand at her feet.

"Pick up your weapon and go, Elta! I better never see you on this property or near my family again."

The Echoes of Her Past

by Sylvia Stein

It was a cold dark night. Maria woke in a pile of sweat soaked sheets, screaming.

"Oh no," she thought to herself as the terror of the nightmare faded. "How long am I going to keep letting these nightmares control my dreams." She sat up and drank some water from the glass she kept beside her bed. She pitted herself – life had become so hard and she wasn't sure how much longer she would be able to deal with it.

As she laid back down, she thought about her life and how it had all led to this moment.

Maria had lived in the city of Austin, Texas all of her life. It was also the place she had met her husband. John was very caring and polite and he did an amazing job of getting her to marry him.

There were friends that though he was too good to be true. Others that though that she should wait until she had made partner in her law firm. But most just wanted her to be happy.

Maria shivered as she recalled how quickly things had changed within their relationship. How easily John could convince her to forgive him.

"I shouldn't have been so gullible!" she cried into her pillow.

Maria recalled her wedding night, how special she had felt spending the night with her new husband. Sadly that feeling ended that very night when John laid his hands on her for the first of many times.

Maria's hands began to tremble as she recalled the first time John Porter showed his true colors.

"Maria, look at the mess you left in this bathroom!" he yelled.

"Oh! I'm sorry," she had said and smiled at John. "I'll pick it up in a minute, okay!"

"What did you say?"

"John, come on. Relax."

She felt John's fist hit her face – she was knocked down to the floor. She laid there in a pool of blood and in pain – stunned. Maria looked up at John. "Why?"

"Baby, forgive me," he said quickly, bending down to comfort her.

"Don't touch me!" she yelled.

Maria got up and looked at herself in the mirror. She couldn't believe what she was seeing. Her lip was cracked and swollen, her left eye was completely shut and was turning blue. But then his hands were on her shoulder, easing her tension away. She forgave him.

Four years later, Maria's heart still beats faster when she thinks about the things that she kept hidden within herself – from herself. She picked up the purple violet from the nightstand that her mother had given her and remembered her words. "Hold on to this, Maria, and it will give you peace and comfort."

Tears once again came over her.

"How could I have let him tell me what to do?" she sobbed.

Her crying caught in her throat when she heard the door knob to her small apartment moving. Immediately her heart was racing and thoughts flew through her head

"No! But it can't be!" she said in a whisper, her body not willing to even breath.

Maria's thoughts ran ahead of her. "I made sure that John would never know where to find me or even that I'm alive. I'm suppose to be free of him – the man who had made my life a walking nightmare."

Her thoughts went back to the night she asked her family for help. Her oldest brother arranged for Maria to begin a new life in another part of the world. Her family helped make John think that she had been lost at sea because of the very high tides that day.

Maria hadn't thought she could go through it, however, when she had recalled the three years of constant abuse, both verbal and physical, and that John was never going to let her live her own life, she had found the strength.

Her new life living abroad in London, England. She found work as a legal secretary – she had even gotten used to her new life, however, she couldn't help but feel homesick from time to time and the nightmares reminded her of what could happen.

The doorknob rattled again and every muscle in her body tensed. The door swung open. She held her breath. Then relief washed over her as Ms. Hannigan, the landlord stepped into the room with a new set of keys.

"Everything okay Mary?" she asked. "I though I heard you calling."

"Yes, everything is fine Ms. Hannigan," Maria said with a calmer voice and even a smile on her face.

Ms. Hannigan handed her the new set of keys for her apartment and left. Maria looked at the purple violet in her hands and realized that maybe, just maybe, peace and comfort might be return to her life.

Flames of Red Make Violet Blue
by Randall Lemon

Lucius loved this land. When he was little, his junkie parents would drive him here to stay with his grandparents. He spent so much time with them; he started to believe his parents didn't want him.

Grandma told him it wasn't true, but each time they retrieved him later, and one day, they didn't come back. Lucius cried himself to sleep wondering what he'd done to make his parents hate him.

His grandparents treated him well, but lived far out in the country so he had no playmates. Grandpa would entertain Lucius by reading stories from the Bible. Lucius liked the stories of the Great Flood, and Sodom and Gomorrah. He tried to make himself useful. He raked leaves in the Fall, gathering them into large piles which Grandpa would set afire. He grew to love the rich aroma of burning leaves. They could spend hours creating a pile of leaves and quickly reduce it to ashes.

Even when not burning leaves, he daydreamed about the conflagrations. Whenever he had the dream, he experienced the sweet satisfaction of fiery destruction. The warmth of the flames made up for his mother, Violet's, lack of warmth.

Years passed and Lucius grew to manhood. Country air, hearty foods, and exercise honed his strength. As his grandparents got older, they became frailer and farm-work fell to Lucius. He didn't mind. Now he was the one to set fire to the leaves and husks and burn the trash.

One day, Grandpa didn't wake up. It was his heart. Lucius was sad at losing Grandpa, but there was work to do. Farms don't tend themselves.

Grandma grew withdrawn. She missed Grandpa even more than Lucius did. She stopped visiting friends. She stopped leaving the farmhouse. Eventually Grandma quit getting out of bed and slipped away.

Lucius was truly alone. He went through the old couple's papers and found some interesting things. There was a will leaving him the farm. He also found letters that his Mother had sent her parents. Lucius read them, finding his father had deserted her. In the letters she asked her parents for money. She included an address in a city, a few hours drive away, where they could send it.

Her letters made Lucius angry. She never asked how he was doing, never even mentioned his name. "That wasn't right." "She wasn't a good woman."

Lucius decided to travel to the city. One day he hopped into Grandpa's Buick. He asked directions from a gas station attendant. As he drove toward the address, the neighborhoods got dirtier and more rundown. He started feeling nervous about talking to her, this woman who put him out like garbage when he was only a boy. Arriving at her address, he stayed in the car uncertain how to approach. Then he saw the door open and some man walked through still buttoning his shirt and handed money to his mother who was dressed only in a slip. Then the man just walked away.

Lucius knew then that his mother was a Jezebel. After a few minutes, he walked up and knocked on the door. Introducing himself, he told her that her parents had died and left her some money and other things. The moment he mentioned the money her eyes lit up.

"I can take you to the farm to get what belongs to you and bring you back."

He told her he was planning to move away and whatever she didn't come and get, he was planning on taking with him. That turned the trick. She dressed hurriedly and accompanied him. Most of the trip was silent, but as they approached the farm, Lucius asked her, "So who was that man I saw coming out of your place just before I got there?"

"None of your business! You spying on me?" snarled Violet. Lucius had been wavering, but the viciousness of her response convinced him.

He took her into the house and showed her some items he claimed her parents had wanted her to have. He could see that she was appraising them for how much money they would bring and how much dope she could by with that money.

Violet asked her son in a sweet voice, "So where is the money you said my parents wanted me to have?"

Lucius licked his lips, "Grandpa turned odd near the end and stopped trusting banks so he took the money and buried it, but he marked the spot with a huge pile of leaves. C'mon I'll show you. I'll just get a shovel so we can dig it up."

They walked to a huge pile of leaves Lucius had pre-pared and when she wasn't looking he hit her with the shovel, not hard enough to kill her, just enough to knock her out.

He got busy with the shovel and dug a deep, narrow hole. He dropped her into it standing up and then filled in the hole around her body leaving only her head above the ground.

When Violet came to, she couldn't budge, the earth was packed tightly around her, but she could talk, "What the hell do you think you're doing?"

"When I was little, you left me here; I'm just doing the same to you. But I'm going to pile a bunch of these leaves around your head first and set fire to them. I'm gonna burn you like God did the sinners of Sodom and Gomorrah and watch your skin turn to ash. And while the fire is still burning, I am just going to walk away. But unlike Lot's wife, I'm not going to make the mistake of turning back to look.

He began packing leaves around Violet's head. Her screams soon turned to coughing, as dirt and leaves got into her mouth and up her nose. When Lucius was satisfied with the pile, he threw some gas on it, tossed a lit match and warmed himself.

"How pleasant burning leaves smell in the Fall!"

Then he walked away.

Lothario

by Tom Russell

No one raised any objections. They all just sat there and stared; their ears open to gossip. Their eyes, closed to the truth. Harris Lothario, a rather handsome, well-dressed young man with a five o'clock shadow that hung daintily on his face, sat at the stand of the poorly-lit courthouse. The district attorney, wearing a suit that covered the injustices of a crooked man in a corrupt judicial system, paced before the judge, before the jury, and before those in the benches whose minds were made well in advance of the trial. All eyes were upon Lothario, burning a hole big enough in him to unload all their anger and disgust.

It was just over seven months ago when Lothario stepped off the train in a town that just so happened to be going through an identity crisis. Jamison Walker, the town's only millionaire and owner of just about every business and building in town, had died without warning. The town was in shock; in mourning of a man who had a giving and compassionate heart—and now was gone.

Harris had looked up-and-down the street. He bent low to pick up his carrying bag, brushed his fingers against his pencil thin moustache and walked toward a hand-painted sign that read: Mama's Café. A small bell on the door announced his entrance. The café was filled with many of the townsfolk, huddled around tables that wobbled and creaked whenever someone walked by. A few greeted Harris with a courteous nod, while others disregarded him and continued on with their small talk. He sat at the only table left, near the window, by the door, and began to eavesdrop.

His smooth French accent was what caught their ears when Harris ordered tea and the house special—fried green tomatoes, corn bread, beans and fried chicken. He ate his meal like it was his last, or so it seemed that way to those sneaking a peek at him, as his knife and fork made scratching noises at the bottom of the tin plate. Just as he swallowed his last bite, a black car, an old Cadillac that was obviously well-cared for, pulled neatly alongside the sidewalk.

The driver, dressed sharply in a hand-stitched suit, stepped out, opened the back door, and out slid the widow Mattie Walker. Just as she reached the café door, the driver turned and chased away several dogs that were ready to leave their scent on the tires. Harris jumped up, opened the door, bowed gracefully and in his most sophisticated accent said: "Mademoiselle, please allow me to be of service to you." Mattie, taken aback by the complete oddity of the gesture, nodded her head and walked past to the only empty table, the table Harris sat at. She was equally surprised when Lothario slid her chair back and then sat across from her.

"My name is Harris. Harris Lothario," he said as he tried to read her expression. "I'm passing through on my way to Florida where I have property. It was getting late so I decided to spend a night in this quaint, quiet town. And your name is, if I may ask?"

Without hesitation she responded: "Mattie Walker. I just buried my husband."

"I'm so sorry," said Lothario. "Your husband must have been a handsome man."

"Why would you say that?" questioned Mattie.

"To live with someone as beautiful as you, he must have been handsome," said Harris in a playful, yet suave manner. Mattie blushed, drank her tea, then left with the townsfolks' eyes on her back.

That night in his motel room, as Harris was preparing to sleep, the phone rang; it was Mattie. "Hello, Harris?" she inquired softly.

"Yes," he responded. "To what do I have the pleasure of hearing your sweet voice."

There was a moment of silence before Mattie responded. "I'm lonely. I know I just laid to rest my wonderful husband, but he was away most of the time. The only other person who's kept me company was Gordon Bigelow, the local district attorney. But that's all he is; just a friend."

"If you can arrange a ride, I can be of comfort and solace to you," he said.

"Good. I'll send a car." She hung up the phone.

That night was the first of many late night trysts between Harris and Mattie until, months later, he simply moved in.

Mattie was the happiest she had ever been. Harris was beside her constantly and within six short months, they got married in a small ceremony at the church near the edge of town. Many of the townsfolk viewed Harris as a gold-digger, but Mattie glowed with joy and contentment.

* * *

The door to the police station had flung open with the force of a desperate man. Harris ran up the stairs and pounded on the desk. "You've got to help me," he shouted desperately. "My wife is missing. I don't know where she is."

The Chief of Police settled him down, took his statement and then sent him home with one condition: Don't leave town.

A week went by, then a month, until a body was found in a shallow grave near the trees a few miles away from town. Everyone assumed it was Mattie Walker-Lothario. The body had begun to crumble into dust; a few violets in the heat of August scattered about. The police arrested Harris on suspicion of murder and the judge ordered the trial date immediately.

The trial had been a mockery and just as the judge began to condemn Lothario to life, the courthouse doors opened, and in walked Mattie.

"Stop! It was him," she yelled to the judge and pointed.

"He kept me locked up in his cabin, but I managed to escape."

She paused and took a deep breath, and in a voice barely audible, said: "Please free my husband."

Harris jumped from the stand and caught Mattie as she collapsed from exhaustion.

Gordon Bigelow slowly began to feel a hole burning in him.

Something Purple

by Linda J Pifer

Stone, the color of lavender, was deepening to a dark something, interpreted only by one inside the cell. He moved further in the tunnel, noting the walls worn by centuries of water rush – smoothing, channeling, cleansing.

Light was far now, leading him straight to it with its rays which punctured and escaped the dark – from depths unknown. He remembered as he traveled toward it; her face, eyes violet with flecks of gold, smooth skin, the smile for him.

Stone widened, its color changed to fluorescent green suddenly, unexpectedly, startling in its brightness, casting a pallor over his hands. Just as suddenly, he was gone from the pallor, further towards the light now, gaining distance from where he began. The cell bumped against something, bouncing him to the wall on his left, then straightening in the path, resuming forward motion. He looked to the right seeing nothing – yet sensing something – and again focused upon the light out ahead. His journey almost finished, hold to the now he thought, hold strong.

It came again on his right, this time he turned to look into it. Nothing visible, yet so tangible and deep he shuddered at the strength of it. It knocked now on the wall – no anger, but its cold seeped into him. He held the stone in his hand, its warmth remaining from her touch upon it as she'd kissed his forehead.

Unspoken, IT arrived to toy with him, preparing to consume and replace all that he was. "You are afraid" it pressed on his brain.

"I am not" he spoke, his lips unmoving.

"Then bargain with me" it demanded.

"I will not" he spoke again from inside.

"Yes you will!" it declared and grew inside his space, blocking the path, bringing back the pallor to him again.

He felt the weakness beginning to hold him, taking him further away from his trajectory. He fought down the panic; it was what IT wanted and he would not give in as long as he had strength. He caught glimpses of the light in the struggle and its rays made holes in IT at every opportunity, creating burns, causing injury, and making IT angrier.

"If you stop now I will stop," IT said, hiding anger from him for a moment in time.

He thought "maybe I should, it will be enough."

From somewhere else she came to him, entering his cell, a breath escaped him as she warmed his space and time. "You must keep fighting!" she said, "You must go the distance."

For her, he renewed his trajectory and spent everything he had left to push the path forward. The light was again fully visible far ahead and its rays surrounded him on all sides, going beyond to where he'd been and drawing him forward into it. The pallor had faded after her words; where was she, he thought as he turned to left and right. She was gone, yet he felt her around him as he gained speed forward.

Pressed instantly backward from him, the Anger spewed forth "Why are you not afraid?"

Because you are insignificant in the Universe, he answered from inside himself. Then IT faded back into the invisible deep dark around him, passing away like dust in a rain shower.

The journey ended. He saw lavender, followed by sunlight from the window in his room, felt it warm his hand as it fell across him. Violet eyes close to his, wide open with flecks of gold and she said "how are you?" Sound so welcome, so fresh, and so wonderful

He found a voice, "I'm okay. Where….?"

"You're in hospital, the surgery, remember? They got all of it. It was encapsulated. You almost left us… you're just fine now," she said with a smile so radiant it hurt his eyes.

Something in his hand caused him to hold up his arm and look. It was a lavender stone, so smooth, deepening to a dark purple at its center.

"It was to help you on your journey" she smiled at him again.

Together

by V. J. M. Christensen

Mel fiddled with his tie. Violet. Like her dress. Where was she? Being late wasn't like Elle at all.

There was a knock on the door. He sighed, relaxing, tension leaving his body,. He walked quickly to the door and opened it. He stopped, baffled. She wasn't there nor was anybody else. He stretched his neck, looking both ways. Not a soul. He looked down. An envelope lay at his feet. Picking it up to examine it, he noticed a strangely familiar seal, which he could not place.

He went inside again, sat by the table and opened the envelope.

"I've got her with me," was all it said. Mel now knew where he recognised the seal from. He grasped his coat, putting it on as he ran to his garage.

As he was about to put on his seatbelt, he realised he didn't know where to go. He was puzzled, which frustrated him. He had no clue about what to do. He went back in the house, sat down again and poured himself a glass of whisky. While taking his coat off he felt a piece of paper. He was surprised to say the least and took it out.

"Well, Melchiore, it seems that you're having a hard time keeping track of your little sweetheart... I can see why you favour living in the Canada - such a beautiful country, and the girl! Oh, and that purple dress... I suggest you go visit a place, where you've been happy lately. -E"

It was written in the too familiar curly handwriting of Erebus. The fair-skinned, light-haired Greek vampire, who'd once been his friend.

Mel reread the note, his fingers tracking the part which mentioned her, the dress.

He was suddenly reminded, very vividly, of the night he met her.

They were on the beach, even though it was winter. Gabrielle hadn't wanted to sit alone in her apartment on Christmas Eve, so she'd gone for a walk. So had he. She'd worn that beautiful violet dress, with a large cream shawl. And it was love at first sight, though he'd never imagined a vampire could fall in love, but Elle was special. They kissed, just as the snow started falling.

"Do you have anything to remind me of you?" she'd asked. "Something I can keep until next time?"

He took his boutonnière, a violet, out of his jacket's buttonhole and gave it to her. "To remember me," he'd whispered before kissing her once more.

He was sitting by his dining-room table, half a year later, fiddling with his tie, the exact colour of that violet, of her dress.

He knew where Erebus had taken her.

Mel immediately left for the beach. He was thinking of her, of how he didn't deserve a woman like Elle, thinking of how he shouldn't have brought her into this life. He was ruining, if not taking, her life, like Erebus had ruined his so many years ago.

However, this wasn't Mel's first experience with Erebus' cruelty.

He had once been a good friend of the vampire.

His mind was flooded with memories of how Erebus had manipulated him to inadvertently betray, and later play a role in the deaths of his parents, his darling baby sister and the girl he'd loved.

Mel could hardly keep calm, thinking of it. Hundreds and hundreds of years had passed, but Mel hadn't forgotten. He had thought he could escape, if not the memories, then the only other of his kind, by traveling away. And it had worked.

Until now.

Why did Erebus do this to him? Mel had never had a bloodlust, while Erebus had one that could never be sated.

Why did he stain every good thing he came into contact with?

He pulled quickly into the parking lot, his tyre hitting the kerb, noticing something stuck on the signpost. He grabbed it, his hands shaking.

"By my estimations, you should arrive here around 4 am. Wasn't that when you had your little Christmas-smooching? I know it is. Wherefore, I know not… Hope you enjoy your stay at this pretty east-facing Canadian beach! Sound like a commercial, eh? Anyway, I've taken the liberty of returning you your flower. -E"

The dried violet was pinned to the note. "Elle," he murmured, "I'm coming!"

Life had been sweet, so sweet, in Canada, with his Gabrielle, but now he had to fight for that sweet life.

He ran down the beach, his body shivering with excitement and tension, his head filled with anger, hate, love, passion. Elle had to be all right, she had to!

Mel saw a figure tied to a post very close to the water.

He ran towards her, screaming.

"Elle. Elle!"

"Thank god, Mel, you've come, you're here! This man, he… he-" she yelled as he was nearing her.

"I know, Elle, I know, but it's all going to be all right, dear."

He was less than two meters from her, when he stopped.

"No!" he screamed, but there wasn't anything to do about it.

The sun rose over the sea, its rays coming up the beach. He staggered forwards as the sun hit him, falling to his knees before her, reaching forward to touch his beloved one last time.

But he was too far away, sitting on his knees, stretching his arms out, his hands, his fingers, to touch her.

The sun, while it shone beautifully, was the most terribly sight either of them had ever seen.

His tears boiled off his skin, and after few seconds, he turned to dust. Gone. Forever.

Gabrielle didn't scream, she couldn't, she was in shock, she could hardly breathe. She collapsed, gliding down as far as her bindings allowed.

Tears streamed down her face, down her violet dress, down her legs. Tears mingled with specks of dust on her right shoe.

Her tears. The dust, which was him.

She. He.

Together.

Ol Jon Quil

by Todd Folstad

"Settle in child and I'll tell you the story of – Jon Quil – quite possibly the meanest and most evil man to ever work the concrete trades in this sector."

Grammy had the best ways to tell stories, like this one, on her lap, with a mug of cocoa and a blanket. She only did it on nights like this when storms grew violent and the sky went every shade of purple from African Violet to Wisteria. When the rains came so hard you could feel the sounds in your body and the winds howl like the hounds of hell themselves. This was such a night.

"Ol Jon," started Grammy, "was the devil himself, folks 'round these parts used to say."

I thought long and hard on that image, as I had seen many pictures and had a bit of difficulty picturing Mr. Quil as the devil. He always looked like a normal man, a ruddy red beard, jeans and a torn, dusty old chambray workshirt. That hardly seemed like the devil to me.

Grammy paused for a drink of her cocoa, then began again, "He was a mean cuss, not to the local children mind you, but to every adult and most visitors of Settler's Bay. He'd fix that blank, dead stare at you and you're blood would run cold. Course, with his one good eye and one glass eye, that stare was something odd to behold."

I asked, "Why did he only have one eye?"

"Well child, that may be the one thing that really made him a mean, mean man. He lost it in a fight at the concrete plant with a traveler who got on the crew for a short term job. Chris Santhemum was a traveler in the old 60's hippie sense of the term. He'd wander from town to town, state to state, hitch-hiking his way up and down the coast looking for work and just 'livin life', as he used to say."

"That doesn't sound so bad," I added.

"No, no it wasn't. But ol Jon just took an instant dislike to him. You see, Jon was a worker from way back, probably never had much of a childhood and didn't like those who had a freedom that he didn't."

"Is it wrong to live life that way Grammy?" I questioned.

"No honey child, it's just the way some folks are made. Never have a home 'cept what they carry on their backs. I suppose it can get lonely, but most of those folks never seem to complain much 'bout it. They just come in, do what they gotta do and then move on."

"So what happened to Mr. Quil's eye?"

"Ol Jon and Chris got into a scrap about some silly piece of equipment at the plant. Ol Jon wanted it scraped, but Chris thought it could be fixed and made useful again. I seem to recall it was for making concrete forms in the shape of pillars and pylons. Useful here on the water for anchoring our docks and mooring ropes for the fishermen."

"So did Chris get it working again?"

"Yes child, he did, and it made Ol Jon mad something fierce. He vowed to have Chris up on charges on account of what was found in the machine."

"What was it Grammy, treasure?"

"No, it was some old clothes and bones. They found some identification in the clothes and it turned out to be a past traveler who had left without even taking his pay. Ol Jon said he just up and left and then the machine was shutdown. Jon said it was broken by the traveler and the plant didn't have the money to fix it."

"How did the man get in there?"

"Lots of folks say that Ol Jon put him in there, locked him in and that's where he died. No one could prove it though, so the police let it drop. Figured a wanderer like that probably didn't have any one to contact anymore, so they just swept it under the rug."

"Chris figured it out, didn't he? He knew what Ol Jon had done, right?"

"That's what most of the townsfolk thought. Anyways, that was over 10 years before Chris showed up, so it had become a kind of local legend. Don't play around the concrete plant or you'll end up dead. It worked well to keep the kids away. Even the teens in the town wouldn't go out there. Then one day, Ol Jon didn't show up for work. Jon being a bit of a drunk, it didn't surprise anyone much, but in truth, he'd never missed a day in over 20 years, so there was some cause for concern. The sheriff went out to his place and found nothing. Door open, no car, no clothing, no food in the house. Empty, like it had just completely vanished. Damnedest thing they'd ever seen.

They questioned everyone at the plant, especially Chris since they had a fight the day before he went missing. Odd thing tho, when they got to the plant, Chris was working the pillar machine. He had fixed it against Ol Jon's wishes and was producing some new pillars for the town's gazebo. He'd heard that the town had commissioned a stone mason to cut and shape new pillars and that the cost was more than the town could afford, so he set about to make them at the plant for less than half the price.

The town fathers were quite happy about that and allowed Chris to finish the work and helped to put his pillars in place for the town."

"Do you think Ol Jon is in one of those pillars Grammy?"

"I can't rightly say honey child, but they do say that on stormy nights, when the sky goes to shades of purple, you can see a glint in one of the pillars that looks like a glass eye, staring out into the heart of the town. Watching and waiting for Chris to return."

"Why for Chris to return? Did he just leave like the other travelers, or something else?"

"Shortly after the gazebo was completed, Chris took over as foreman at the plant and ran it to record profits for himself and the town. After a few years, he had enough for his own house-boat, he bought it and now lives the good life out on the shore. He comes in occasionally to check on the gazebo, to treat the pillars with weather resistant chemicals and to say hello to all the workers who now enjoy a much happier life.

"So you remember now honey child, don't you go play out at the concrete plant, or you may get the stare from the 'glass eye of Ol Jon. Go to sleep now and know that Grammy loves you and I'll be here when you wake."

They Paved Paradise - Didn't They

by Gene Hilgreen

Last night I snuck out, hours after everyone went to sleep, I'd been doing this all summer. It was my job to wake up my friends, and we would cruise the streets of good old WI until the sun began to break the horizon. The back door to the Captree Day Camp indoor pool was open that night (ok, maybe it wasn't), so we decided to have some fun. The cops came, one guy got caught, and my Mom was sitting on my bed – when I snuck back in through the window.

"You're grounded – two weeks."

"I hate you."

"Make that the rest of the summer. Think about it, we'll talk tomorrow."

The door vibrated when I kicked it closed. She was still babbling when she left. If it was the future, I would have clicked my magic everything controller and my three flat screen TV's would be on, Rock and roll music would be blasting, and I wouldn't hear my mom screaming. I would be texting my girlfriend Violet and complaining.

But I can't do any of that—it's nineteen sixty-nine—the summer of love.

I'm lucky I have a black and white TV, and the only reason it gets the NY Met's game, is because I have a wire spliced to the antenna running out my window, and up the chimney.

My mom grew up on the mean streets of New York in the 30's, her family was connected (if you get my drift), and there wasn't anything she hadn't done by the time she was fifteen. She was seventeen when she married my dad, days before he shipped out for the USMC boot camp at Parris Island. She was determined to raise me honorably, and grounded me every time I steered down the wrong path.

Later the next day, there is a knock on my door; it must be the wicked witch.

"What?"

"I bought you a six-pack of your favorite…Colt 45."

"Thanks, I still hate you. I left my pay envelop on the counter."

"Can I come in?"

"No!"

The door to my bedroom opened.

"Boo!"

There stood my Mom, her hair dyed platinum blond, looking all Marilyn Monroe—damn she looked beautiful.

"Listen, when I was your age, I was married and had two jobs."

"Yeah well, I'll be seventeen next month and when I'm eighteen—I'm out of here. No more women telling me, what I can and can't do."

My mother left my room laughing. "Violet is here… you going to tell her… or do you want me to?"

"I'll tell her."

Violet is fifteen going on twenty-four, her parents grew up on the tough streets too, but Violet gets away with murder. She's hot and my mother is afraid she will steer me wrong. God forbid that we might be having sex.

"Kathy told me you can't go," Violet said.

I told you she was all grown up, she calls my Mom, Kathy. She also happens to be my Mom's shortstop.

"Yeah well, my Dad says I have to work next Friday and Saturday morning."

I lied—my Dad said I could go, but I'm not going to tell her.

"Well I'm going; I'm not missing this for nothing. My friends and I are going to head there Wednesday, and stake out our spot. It will probably go down as the greatest event in our lifetime."

Violet gave me a passionate kiss, and left—it was the last time I ever saw her.

Friday night after the Met game, I decide to watch the news that follows. The field reporter is talking about Arlo Guthrie. And they flash to him on stage.

He says, "I don't know, like, how many of you can dig how many people there are, man. Like, I was rapping to the fuzz, right? Can you dig it? Man, there's supposed to be a million and half people here by tonight. Can you dig that? New York State Throughway is closed, man."

With that, my mother walks into my bedroom; she's a big Met fan too.

"If you still want to go after work tomorrow, you can go."

I told you she was mean. "Thanks Mom, you're the best."

Forget about the Throughway being closed, we were three miles from the Throgs Neck Bridge, and not moving anywhere. I got out of the VW Beetle. "Have fun guys, I'm going home." I crossed the divider and stuck out my thumb, with my bandana around my head and a Hendrix T-shirt on, it took about an hour before someone picked me up.

Forty years later—

I'm on Route 55, approaching 17B, and I see the sign for White lake. Like magic, I transform to that sixteen-year old kid again. I'm almost there. I make a left on 17B, about a quarter of a mile on the right is Hector's Last Chance Saloon. I pull in to catch my breath and get some ice. Remnants of the greatest event of my lifetime are positioned on both sides of the parking lot. The stand from where Wavy Gravy and the Hog Farm fed hundreds of thousands of Hippies now stands at Hectors. The famous painted bus and every sign from the magical event they could find—hung proud for all to see. Several Hippies are building a thirty-foot diameter fire pit, a fire already blazing in the middle. At least twenty mobile campers are parked along the road, and hundreds of tents are setup in the field. The event is four days away, but that didn't stop these people from reliving their past.

I walk out of the bar with a bag of ice and get into my Van. A couple of sixty plus-year old Hippies are smoking a joint by the pit.

"Hey son," an older Hippie says. "Where you going… you just got here?" He walks over and introduces himself. "I'm Jerry Hector, come on and take a walk with me."

We tour his little piece of paradise. He points to a statue of Jimi Hendix made of sand. "You know who that is right."

"Sure do," I say. "Jimi died on my twentieth birthday. Hey listen Hector, I've to get my ticket, but I'll be back—promise."

Later that day I'm walk the great fields, where a half-a-million people enjoyed three days of fun and music. I return every day for the next four days, and hang with Hector and the children of God—the lucky ones who make the trek every year. I meet Michael Lang the original producer, Grace Slick, Country Joe, Mountain. In fact, Leslie West of Mountain marries the love of his life that night, right on the stage where he performed forty years earlier.

I had lived Woodstock through every form of media available for the previous forty years. The fortieth was great, but could anything ever match the first. For me it was close enough. Woodstock is not a place, it's a beautiful state of mind, just ask Michael Lang. He told me, "live it, feel it, and be it."

I've made the trek to Yasgur's Farm and Hector's Last Chance saloon every year since for Woodstock weekend, somewhere near August 15th.

For three days—politics and everything else takes a back seat. Make that four—I never miss Hippie Thanksgiving the Thursday before. It's a time for peace, love, and music.

A few weeks after the Fortieth Reunion, Violet found me on Facebook. She had hooked up with Wavy Gravy and the Hog Farm and moved to Arizona. She's still a hippie, and so am I—maybe.

Nothing lasts forever. Someone is always looking to make a buck. A monument now stands at the site.

Most of the garden is gone ... but it will never be forgotten.

They paved paradise – now it's a parking lot. And castles made of sand – fall in the sea – eventually.

The Luck of the Shamrocks
by Lena M. Pate

Around the quaint cottage was a garden filled with
flowering bushes and edged around all with the deep violet
leaves of the Oxalis. Partial to her purple clover with the
dainty white flowers, Alana could be generally found weed-
ing and feeding her colorful garden. Alana decorated her
front yard with ceramic leprechauns and a bench circled a
huge old oak where she sat in the afternoons spinning tales
of Ireland to the neighborhood children on their way home
from school.

"Once upon a time there was a mean ogre who never
wore a smile. He would sit on the only bridge from the
village to the local's farms and torment the children as they
went to school each day. He would demand in his garbled
voice, "Children who play must always pay" and then stole
their lunches to cross his bridge."

"What happened if they couldn't pay the troll," Jeffrey
asked Alana hugging his dog Rusty to his chest.

"Well, sometimes he wouldn't let them cross. Other times he would torment them until they were late for school. Even worse, he would hold them under his bridge until dark and make them walk home alone."

"What did their families do about the ogre," asked little Mary.

"Why that's a tale for another day," she said to the groans of the children. But they waved goodbye and high-tailed it home. Being children, some of them ran across her neighbor's lawn which made him very mad.

"You stupid kids with your stupid pets. Tearing up my grass and letting them do their business on my lawn. I will fix you I will" he shouted, shaking a fist at their departing backs.

"This is entirely your fault Miss Alana. I blame you for them making this mess. If you would let them go home like they should, they would not be over here wasting time listening to your silly stories about fairies, leprechauns and other such nonsense."

The vile little man that was yelling went by the name of Finlay Giles. Finlay also took pride in his yard but hated animals and people alike. He kept a perfectly maintained lawn with sculptured trees and bushes.

Late that evening, he planted sticker bushes between Alana's yard and his. He erected a metal fence with sharp points to block out unwanted visitors.

The next afternoon, Jeffrey fell off his bike into the sticker bushes. Alana took the boy inside, cleaning the cuts and giving the boy a cookie to dry his tears.

That evening when she saw Mr. Giles she yelled across to him. "Your bushes are dangerous and hurt a child today."

"Serves the brat right, he deserves what he got. Anyone who trespasses will pay a tall price."

"We'll see who pays the tall price Mr. Giles." Alana threatened.

The next morning Mr. Giles discovered that all of his sticker bushes had been cut down.

Alana looked up and waved from her garden of shamrock. "Top of the morning to you Finlay. I hope you slept well last night."

"Why you , you witch you. I'll have you arrested, you'll see"

But when the police came they could only take his statement because there was no proof as to who had chopped the shrubbery down.

Alana told the police about the boy who had been hurt. "I don't know what happened to his bushes but I can say that I'm not sad to see them gone." After the police left, she smiled at Finlay and then prepared for the children to stop by for story time.

The next day Alana came out to work in her gardens only to find all of her beautiful violet shamrocks had been dug up and destroyed. Not one single delicate flower survived the massacre. She looked next door and there stood Mr. Giles with a smirk across his face.

"I told you I'd make you pay!" he shouted, waving his newspaper over his head like a banner.

That evening a horrendous storm hit, shaking the trees, lightning and thunder clashing, tagging the ground with all its fury. Windows shook, the ground quaked and neighbors huddled in their homes praying to stay safe until morning. Streets flooded carrying debris of branches, trashcans, and furniture in its wake. Hail rained down covering the lawns and winds so strong that it uprooted trees and destroyed fences. In the morning heads started to peer out of the windows checking on their properties and that of their neighbors. Only one home had been destroyed by the storm. After the police and firemen arrived they sifted through the ashes finding no signs that anyone had been at home.

"That is a blessing because everything is gone. The house was burnt by lightning, the grass destroyed by the hail and even his fence is no longer standing." One neighbor noticed.

"Yes but where would he go?"

"Maybe he had family; after all, he was getting quite old."

"Well I can't say I'm sad to see him gone but I would never wish him harm." Said another woman as she led her youngsters back inside.

The next time the children came over to Alana's house one of them asked her to finish the story about the troll.

"Well one night there was a terrible storm like the one we just had. When the children started off for school the next day, they noticed that the bridge had been destroyed in the storm. They went back to get their parents who decided the bridge would have to be rebuilt because the wood was nothing but ashes."

"Did the troll burn up with the bridge?" Sammy asked.

"No dear, that was the strange thing. When the people cleared the area where the bridge had stood they found that the troll had turned to stone." Alana turned and looked at the new stone troll that graced her freshly planted shamrocks at the corner of her house and smiled.

Alone?

by Douglas G Clarke

Crack! Crunch! Melissa smashed against the side of the carriage as it pitched to the right. Pain shot through her arm and the sound of the horses whinnying filled the quiet evening.

"Sorry miss," came the voice of the driver. "One of our wheels broke. Are you alright?"

Melissa struggled to poke her head out of the small window. "I'm fine, James. Can you fix it?"

James jumped down from the carriage. "I'll fetch a cartwright." And with that, he turned and ran.

Melissa watched as he left the pool of light cast by the carriages lamps and disappeared into the darkness beyond. Lost to sight, she listened to his echoing footfalls fade into silence.

Alone, Melissa became aware of her surroundings – the plush purple fabric, the golden cords, and the maple paneling of her box in the darkness. Outside there were no colors

- only shades of black. The squares of the cobblestone road, the shadow cast by a wall in the light from a sliver of moon above, hewn granite blocks of the walls stretching into the star spatted blackness of the sky.

Melissa pulled away from the window and wrapped her cloak tightly around herself despite the warmness of the evening. The minutes seemed to tick by slowly as she watched the second hand move around the face of her pocket-watch, and more than once she chides herself when she found her fingernails between her teeth.

At first she thought it was the wind, but as it grew, the moaning caused the hairs on her neck to rise. Melissa peered into the darkness – she saw dark shapes moving in the blackness, the moaning seemed to come from each of them and none of them. Opening the door and slipping onto the street, Melissa lifted one of the carriage's lamps from its holder and backed away from the creatures of the night.

She turned and walked quickly – leaving the pool of light cast by the carriage – now trapped in her own five foot pool. Stepping onto the sidewalk, her fingers found the rough stone wall of a building – she followed it. No light shown from the windows of the buildings on either side of the street. No sound joined that of her footsteps and the moans following her.

The wall ended. Across the street a cathedral dominated the sky – its flying buttresses arcing towards heaven, its buttresses each housing a saint, and silhouetted against the starry sky, a beast.

Melissa hesitated, but only for a moment. The moaning behind her grew louder and was joined by a scraping. She hurried across the road and into the shadows of the cathedral. Despite, or perhaps because of, her lantern, the shadows between the buttresses seems even blacker than black.

She jumped when a rat scurried from one pool of inky blackness to another. Her heart pounded in her ears. Her hand trembled as she reached to the stone wall for support. Slipping into the alcove formed by the first two buttresses, Melissa lowered the hood of her lamp, plunging herself into night.

The moan continued from around the corner, the scraping as well, but now a scraping also came from above. Frozen for a moment, Melissa struggled to make her body obey. Slowly, too slowly, she peered around the corner. A black shape in the night approached, be it a beast or a man she could not decide, but it was crossing the street towards her.

She glanced up at a new scraping sound. The stone guardians on their perches were gone. "Run" was all her mind was telling her, so she ran. From buttresses to buttresses, keeping to their shadows, somehow the space between them feeling safer.

A scream pierced the night. Melissa turned and ran – straight into a buttress. The lantern smashed into the wall. Its shutters broke free and clattered to the ground – filling the alcove with light. Acting like she held a snake, she flung it to the ground. It hit with a crash and spilled its guts onto the stone – flame quickly followed. She ran blindly into the night.

Ahead she saw another figure – wings in its silhouette – and slid to a stop and then ducked into the blackness of an alcove. She sat in the corner – legs pulled up against her chest – waiting for the end to come. The moaning and scrapping grew closer, then they were upon her. A man's shape appeared – framed by the opening – a knife in his hand.

Melissa screamed when she saw the gash in his overcoat and unmistakable dark spot in the moonlight. The man raised the knife, then the moonlight was blotted out as a winged shape fell from the sky. His scream joined hers as the two shapes became one.

Abruptly his scream ended and Melissa opened her eyes to see the man's shape lying on the ground and that of a beast upon him. Neither moved – not a breath –– not a quiver. She watched in horror as the two were locked in unending mortal combat. Unable to move and unable to watch any longer, she closed her eyes and cried.

The sound of men running and dogs baying brought hope back to her soul. She dared to look again and saw only the man – unmoving. When the others arrived and she was once again bathed in light, she saw that the man and all he wore were stone – all, but a glass jar that lay broken by his waist, its contents a human heart and violet water – spreading out like it was his own.

Melissa looked up and saw the silhouette of the beasts looking down on her from their unmoving perches and wondered at the sight.

Afterwords

The Countryman
D C Mills

Some stories are older than anyone can remember.

Stories of heroes slaying dragons, winning the treasure and the princess.

Jason and the Golden Fleece is one of these stories, with Jason's uncle Pelias cast as The Villain who sent Jason on this intended suicide mission.

But what were Pelias' motives? Surely, he was not a cartoon villain, intent on doing evil to an unsuspecting young man. These days, we want all our characters to be 3-dimensional, to be realistically motivated.

So, this story is an attempt to look into Pelias and see what happened to make him act as he did.

All Done, Well Done
David Russell

Summer is one of my favorite seasons of the year, and much of my life has been lived where the four seasons are nearly as certain as death and taxes.

In my former vocation as a Medical Transcriptionist, I was occasionally impacted by those lives which were reported to have a bit more hardship much like those reflected in my story. The days of the nuclear family no longer exist for over half of those who marry and start a family, and believe one's writing has to be in tune with today's cultural realities. The theme of August Violets taps into my appreciation of summer, and the story of my main character, Lilly, taps into my care and compassion for fellow human-beings living with a cultural reality that seems rather painful.

Small Purple Catalyst
Suzanne H Ferris

I do enjoy a good writing prompt. Being given a theme, a crazy idea or my favourite of all – take three things and turn them into a story.

Small Purple Catalyst came from the 'Violet or Something Purple' prompt for the August story.

I let the idea stew for a while, pondering on how perhaps one small thing could evoke powerful memories – good or bad.

But wouldn't it be spooky, shivery, shaky-quaky, if the same little thing could set off unforeseen circumstances!

I write novels, short stories and children's books as Suzanna Stanbury, this is the only story written under my real name of Suzanne H Ferris as I use that for editing, ghost-writing and proof-reading services, but hey ho, let the old girl have a chance, is what I say.

Alone In The City
Helen Blenkinsop

I've worked in the City of London and seen the stress it causes. In fact, there was a sad case of a young man who died after working three nights in a row without any sleep. The "hero" of this tale smokes to get by. There are worse vices. At least, his habit is legal, and by the end of the story, we know that he may one day break it. He has turned the corner.

I think I'm free of cigarettes too, but for a while, they seemed to feature in all my writing. My first novel, Up In Smoke, was a thriller about Big Tobacco. Anyways, this story is the last one about smoking – I promise...

Zoe and the Dragon
Rebecca Lacy

Zoe and the Dragon was born out of my feeling that there is more to this world than meets the eye. Who knows what magic we might see if we keep an open mind?

When I'm hiking in the woods with dense foliage forming a canopy overhead, and the sounds of civilization are replaced by a furtive rustling of leaves, it is easy to be transported to a time and place where anything is possible – even dragons. That is where the story was born.

I've always been a big fan of dragons and feel that they have gotten a bum rap for centuries. Yet we can clearly see that they are, in fact, good and useful creatures as evidenced by Pete, Toothless, Puff and others. *Zoe and the Dragon* is one more illustration that not all dragons are monsters.

I hope you enjoy the story.

Winning Violets
Mike Boggia

An old mission, now a National Monument, south of
Tucson, AZ, shelters long flower-beds of large, beautiful
light purple violets under the patio roof. Coming from
the northeast, it is interesting to see violets thriving in the
excessive heat. It became my hero's garden. Observations in
the waiting room of my eye doctor built a plot for the story.
Macular degeneration can't stop her, or me.

Turned to Stone
Arlene Lagos

This was closely-based on a true story about my life. The bus, the panic, the agoraphobia. It was a life-altering event and it left me very depressed for a very long time. But then I decided to make a change, try a new path, switch up my life and try and see the beauty in the world. *Turned to Stone* is about seeing the color in a world of darkness.

Shadowdeep
Alli Vaughan

Shadowdeep is part of a project of mine that delves quite a bit further into the dark lives of the shadow creatures. It's some of my best writing and I'm very proud of it. I don't think we as writers give ourselves enough credit, but some pieces are very special to each of us and this is one in particular.

Violet Berries
Lynn Johnston

I enjoy becoming acquainted with the other members in the 750 group as we read each other stories and offer positive feedback. It helps to hear their words of encouragement and allows me to do the same for others. I also am delighted to extend my connections with Linked-In.

I then became inspired to write *Violet Berries* based on my own love for berry picking. Since the color "violet" was the chosen theme, it was an obvious choice for the color of the berries.

Elta's Folly
Lynette White

With this story I returned to my true passion, fantasy. To a world of druids and mystical connections to the very powers of nature itself.

Young Erianna must make a decision. Does she run and hide, or choose to stand and fight. Choosing to fight will mean she must square off against the much older, and more seasoned, Elta.

Erianna learns she has an inner strength she never knew she possessed. Elta makes a critical mistake in assuming the young girl is no threat to her. She learns far to late that Erianna will stop at nothing to save those she loves.

May each of us be as brave if we must protect those dear to our hearts.

The Echoes of Her Past
Sylvia Stein

I wrote this story about a woman who is trying to re-build her life after escaping her abusive husband. This story recounts her experience with him and how she made the mistake of marrying him and how she regrets her mistake.

I wanted to write this story for all the women out there that have suffered this type of abuse by someone they love. Sadly this story hits a bit close to home. I have had friends go through this and I wanted to tell their story.

Flames of Red Make Violet Blue
Randall Lemon

We were given the opportunity to write about a violet, a terrible antagonist and something living that turns to ash or stone.

In my story I chose to deal with a person named Violet. Much of what I put into my story was inspired by the Biblical story of Sodom and Gomorrah and the terrible justice that God visited upon the sinners there. As to the terrible antagonist, I leave it to the reader to decide just who the antagonist really was.

Lucius commits a truly heinous act. Certainly he is a pyromaniac and worse. But Violet is a junkie who abandons her child and only reenters his life to get money to buy more drugs.

So, who is the villain and who is the victim?

Pick on or combine

Mitigating circumstances! One often hears that term in news articles about people on trial for serious offences such as murder.

But is there such a thing? Are there just and reasonable motives to commit murder, let alone, to commit a murder in a truly gruesome fashion?

Many people grow up in less than ideal families and yet mature into fine, law-abiding citizens who exhibit the most Christianlike traits. They love their fellow men and support charities to help the unfortunate. Still others find themselves on trial for crimes but claim by way of defense that it was their upbringing that is really responsible for their criminal behavior years later.

Most people would agree that self-defense is a logical reason for killing someone. They try to kill you, but you kill them first. It's like revenge for something that didn't quite happen. How long is the statute of limitations on such a self-defense killing? If someone hurt you when you were young, are you justified in killing them years later?

Lucius escapes being raised by unsavory parents and instead is brought up by kind people who teach him to love the land and the lessons taught in the Bible. Certainly there could be no mitigating circumstances that would turn him into a cold-blooded killer. Right?

Lothario
Tom Russell

Life has a strange way of making things work out for some, even if, at times, their intent is otherwise. Harris Lothario was a rambler who just happened to be in the right place at the right time. In this instance, when two forces meet (loneliness and opportunity), the results are surprising.

Harris's last name, Lothario, is described as a man whose chief interest is seducing women.

Will he ever find what he's looking for?

Something Purple
Linda J Pifer

This story came straight out with no forethought or planning; the goal was to utilize a totally different style of writing and use fantasy to get inside the mind of a man fighting a serious illness.

Looking at the finished piece, I realize years spent in a hospital career greatly influence my writing; knowing the dreams people conjure up during anesthesia and understanding the monster that cancer is, "IT" embodies the insidious character of cancer attempting to take over a life. The man reaches inside himself to tap a renewable strength previously unknown, which enables him to remain steadfast and claim his victory.

Reality at last brings him to the surface, out of the neverland of the unconscious mind to the sun's warmth. His loved one is there waiting to greet him; it was she who placed the healing amethyst crystal in his hand as an amulet to overcome fear during the dangerous journey.

There are many who believe in the healing powers of crystals and those who believe in the healing power of one God. Believing is their strength and for those battling right now against "IT" may you be blessed by healing.

This story came straight out with no forethought or planning; the goal was to utilize a totally different style of writing and use fantasy to get inside the mind of a man fighting a serious illness.

Together
V. J. M. Christensen

This is a story about vampires.

This is a sad story.

This is a love story.

This is a story which romanticises vampires.

I really enjoyed writing this story, which was the first I wrote about Melchiore and Gabrielle, but not the last.

I've written short stories about them since I wrote this, and I will probably write more short (or perhaps "long") ones in the future.

If you're thinking, "What happens next?" check out the next *A Giant Tale* anthology – their story hasn't ended yet!

Ol Jon Quil
Todd Folstad

Ol Jon Quil is a look into the mystery of a man who lived in the shadows until he was able to step into the light, and then become transparent again.

It is a view of how our pasts and our personal biases can intrude on our lives and imprint on our futures. I can and will add to this character study over time and may revisit Mr. Quil in the future.

Working within the framework of the Fiction Writers Guild and the Writers 750 groups has been a great way to unlock some of the newer parts of my writing background. By taking part in these 'contests', I've been able to use them as an exercise in forced writing, to make me work even when the flow isn't going. Of all of the stories that I've composed for these monthly events, which have helped me to hone my craft and by exposed me to fresh ideas and tools that I may never have uncovered, *Ol Jon Quil* is one of my favorite character studies.

They Paved Paradise–Didn't They
Gene Hilgreen

The Writers 750 Group run by Heather Schultz was a Godsend to me. It gave me the chance to hone my writing skills while interacting with other members–who are now like family–on a wide range of topics.

I'd also like to thank the editors, who are part of our group, and helped make this anthology a reality.

I had some fun drawing on real life experiences while meeting the short story theme, and selected criteria with They Paved Paradise. I hope you enjoyed it.

Peace–

The Luck of the Shamrocks
Lena M. Pate

The Luck of the Shamrocks came to me while sitting in my private little garden surrounds by my flowers and Oxalis. Oxalis are beautiful purple shamrocks that open to the daylight and close to rest at night. Their small flowers add a delicacy that encourages protection. Also included in my garden are several garden gnomes adding gaiety to the mix. When I read the requirements for the Violet Hopes Challenge, the story came to life before me. I could picture a woman tending her gardens and devising stories for the neighborhood children, giving them something to look forward to each day. But for all good there is also evil and the battle that must take place to resolve and return the peace can be a devastating journey.

"Imagination is the gift I wish to bestow to my grandchildren. One can never be lonely when your mind is full of friends and adventures."

Alone?
Douglas G Clarke

Alone is my first attempt at writing a horror short story. Focusing on description and trying to make the reader feel the uneasiness that Melissa was feeling was my approach going in. I knew I wanted to include gargoyles as soon as I read the part of the prompt, "living flesh to stone."

As I started to write, I decided that I would go back to the original reason gargoyles were put on buildings – to protect them and keep away the evil spirits. With that decision made it quickly followed that the evil in my story would be another human.

I tried to play the unknown threat that was following Melissa with the fears of what lay ahead as she saw the statues above. I tried to build suspense by not reveling the details of the threat following her and not revealing that the gargoyle was going to save her.

Thank you for reading *Violet Hopes*, we hope you enjoyed it. If you would like to find out more about the book and its authors, please visit www.agoodtale.com

Also, look for our other books
Trash to Treasure
Of Past and Future